STRIDER

BEVERLY CLEARY is one of America's most popular authors. Born in McMinnville, Oregon, she lived on a farm in Yamhill until she was six and then moved to Portland. After college, she became the children's librarian in Yakima, Washington. In 1940, she married Clarence T. Cleary, and they are the parents of twins, now grown.

Mrs. Cleary's books have earned her many prestigious awards, including the American Library Association's Laura Ingalls Wilder Award, presented in recognition of her lasting contribution to children's literature. Her *Dear Mr. Henshaw* was awarded the 1984 John Newbery Medal, and her *Ramona and Her Father* and *Ramona Quimby, Age 8* have been named Newbery Honor Books. In addition, her books have won more than thirty statewide awards based on the votes of her young readers. Her characters such as Henry Huggins, Ellen Tebbits, Otis Spofford, Beezus and Ramona Quimby, as well as Ribsy, Socks, and Ralph S. Mouse, have delighted children for more than a generation.

Beverly Cleary

STRIDER

Illustrated by
Paul O. Zelinsky

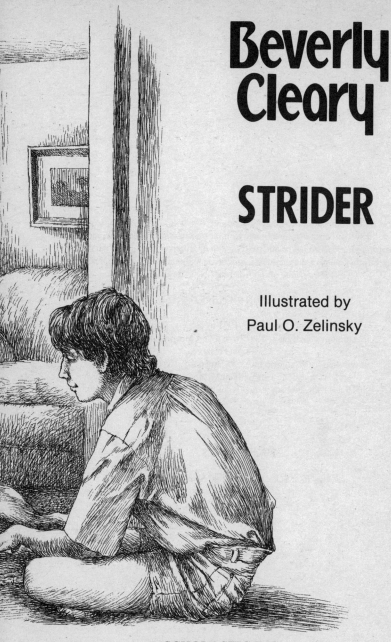

SCHOLASTIC INC.
New York Toronto London Auckland Sydney
Mexico City New Delhi Hong Kong

ISBN 0-439-14804-9

31 30   9/0

Printed in the U.S.A.   40

First Scholastic printing, September 1999

For Malcolm

From the Diary of Leigh Botts

June 6

This afternoon, as Mom was leaving for work at the hospital, she said for the millionth time, "Leigh, please clean up your room. There is no excuse for such a mess. And don't forget the junk under your bed."

I said, "Mom, you're nagging. I'm going to Barry's house."

She plunked a kiss on my hair and said, "Room first, Barry second. Besides, where would the world be without nagging mothers? Everything would go to pieces."

Maybe she's right. Things are pretty deep in my room. I hauled all the rubbish out from under my bed. In the midst of all the old socks,

1

school papers, models that have fallen apart, paperback books (one library book—oops!), and other stuff, I found the diary I kept a couple of years ago when I was a mixed-up kid in the sixth grade. Mom had just divorced Dad and moved with me to Pacific Grove, better known as P.G., where I was a new kid in school, which wasn't easy.

I sat there on the floor reading my diary, and when I finished, I continued to sit there. What had changed?

Dad still drives his tractor-trailer rig, lives mostly on the road, and is late with his child support checks or forgets them. I don't often see him, but I don't get as angry about this as I did in the sixth grade. I no longer feel like crying, but I still hurt when he doesn't telephone when he said he would. Whenever I see a big rig, excitement shoots through me until I see Dad isn't the driver. I wish—oh well, forget it.

Mom has finished her vocational nurse course and works at the hospital from three to eleven because that shift pays more than the daytime shift. Mornings she studies to become a registered nurse so she can earn more money. We still live in what our landlady called our "charming garden cottage" but I call a shack. Mom is looking for an apartment, but so far no luck.

Twice a week I mop the floor at Catering by Katy, where Mom used to work before she got her license. Katy gives me good things to eat. I like earning my own spending money, but I feel I could use the squares of Katy's linoleum for a checkerboard in my sleep.

Mom, who used to think TV was one of the greatest evils of the universe, finally had our set repaired because my grades were good and she no longer felt TV would rot my brain and leave me twiddling my shoelaces. At first I watched everything until I got bored and cut back to news and animal programs. Then I began to feel that every lion on the Serengeti must have his own personal hairdresser. That left the news, which sometimes worries me. If I see a truck accident with the tractor hanging over the edge of a bridge, or tons of tomatoes spilled on a freeway, I can hardly breathe until I see the driver isn't Dad.

One part of my diary made me smile, the part about wanting to be a famous author like Boyd Henshaw someday. Maybe I do, maybe I don't, but I'm glad that when I wrote to him, he said I should keep a diary.

I worry about what I'm going to do with my life, and so does Mom. Dad is probably too busy worrying about meeting his deadline with a trailer load of lettuce before it rots to even think of me. Or maybe he is wasting his time playing video games at some truck stop.

Until the last sentence, I enjoyed writing this. Maybe I'll go back to writing in composition books, but not every day, just once in a while, like now, when I feel like writing something.

The gas station next door has stopped ping-pinging, which means it's after ten o'clock. Mom gets home about eleven-thirty, and my room is still a mess. No problem. Except for books and my diary, I'll dump everything in the trash.

I just remembered. I forgot about Barry.

June 7

Today I have something important to write about! The summer fog was so low the whole world seemed to drip. Mom went to class, and our shack was so lonely, I climbed the hill to see Barry. I like to go to his big old house, built on a slope so that it has a view of the bay when the fog lifts. Everything in the house is shabby and comfortable. There is a smell of good things cooking. Barry's stepmother, Mrs. Brinkerhoff, is plump, but she doesn't worry about it the way Mom's friends worry about gaining one teeny ounce.

Barry's house is full of cats, hamsters in cages, and little sisters. I once saw a tortoise under the couch, but I have never seen it again. Sometimes a grandmother is there. She knits sweaters out of beautiful soft yarns in wild designs she makes up as she goes along. Barry says she sells them to an expensive boutique for a lot of money. Watching her needles move so quickly in and out of beautiful yarns fascinates me.

The basic Brinkerhoffs are the parents, Barry, and five little sisters. Two girls belong to Barry's father, two to his stepmother, and the little one, who crawls and likes to play peekaboo around corners, belongs to both parents. Sometimes the girls seem like more than five because their friends come over, and they all dress up in old clothes Mrs. Brinkerhoff keeps in a big box.

This morning a bunch of girls were kneeling on chairs around the kitchen table, popping corn in the electric corn popper. When they dumped it out in a bowl, Barry and I reached for some.

The girls tried to slap our hands away. "This isn't for eating," one of them said. "This is for shrinking."

That stopped us. Whoever heard of shrinking popcorn?

The girls were busy dropping perfectly good popcorn into a bowl of water, one piece at a time, to watch it shrink until nobody would eat it except maybe a hamster.

"That's a stupid thing to do," Barry told the girls.

"It is not," said the oldest sister. Betsy I think is her name. "We are performing a scientific experiment to prove that popcorn has memory.

6

Drop it in water, and it remembers it is supposed to be little and hard instead of big and fluffy."

Barry and I helped ourselves to more popcorn. "You're being mean to popcorn," said one of the girls, which made me wonder what popcorn remembered when I chewed it.

Barry and I went to his room to work on a model of an antique car with many little parts. If we put glue on one piece and couldn't find where it belonged right away, the plastic melted, and the piece wouldn't fit. That happened a couple of times. Then I got glue on the hood. When I tried to wipe it off, the shine wiped off, too. The funny part was, I didn't much care.

I looked at Barry, and he looked at me. I could see we both had the same thought at the same time: *we had outgrown models.* Without saying anything, we threw the car pieces into the wastebasket, and as we went through the kitchen, we snatched some more popcorn.

Here comes Mom's car, it's almost midnight, I'm supposed to be asleep, and I haven't even come to the good part. I'll write more about today tomorrow.

June 8

Back to yesterday. There are so many places our moms won't let us hang around, like the Frostee Freeze and the video arcade, that we headed for the beach, not for any special reason. The beach was just a place to go. The damp air gave us goose bumps below our cut-offs. Fog dripping off the eucalyptus trees made them smell like old tomcats.

The beach was so gray and chilly the only person around was a rugged old man we call Mr. President because he is always saying if he were president he would make a few changes in this country. He patrols beaches and parks, dragging two gunnysacks, one for broken glass and beer bottles, the other for aluminum cans, so kids won't cut their feet. Some people think he's nutty because he lives in an old bread truck, but we don't. Sometimes we help him.

At the foot of the steps to the beach, beside the seawall, a dog was sitting in the soft sand. He was tan with a few white spots and a white mark in the center of his face. He looked strong for a medium-sized dog.

"Hi, dog," I said and thought of my ex-dog Bandit and the fun we used to have before the divorce, when Mom got me and Dad got Bandit.

This dog looked worried and made little whimpering noises.

Mr. President came dragging his gunnysacks through the sand. "Dog's been sittin' there since yesterday," he said. "No collar, no license, no nothin'. Just sits there in sorrow."

"Come on, fella," I said to the dog and patted my knee.

The dog didn't move. I scratched his chest where Bandit liked to be scratched. This dog looked up at me with his ears laid back and the saddest look I have ever seen on a dog's face. If dogs could cry, this dog would be crying hard.

"Come on, dog," said Barry. The dog wagged his docked tail. It wasn't a happy wag. It was an anxious wag. Dogs can say a lot with their tails, or what people let them keep of their tails. If he still had a tail, it would be between his legs.

"Seems like somebody told him to stay, so he's staying," said Mr. President. "If he sits much longer, that dog jailer will come along and haul him off to the dog bastille."

"Come on, boy," I coaxed. The dog didn't budge.

"If I were running this country, I would hang everyone who dumps animals," said Mr. President and went back to picking up beer bottles people leave on the beach.

Barry and I slogged through the dry sand to the wet sand, both of us hoping the dog would follow, but he didn't. I couldn't forget the look on that dog's face. I know what it feels like to be left behind, so I probably have the same look on my face when Dad and Bandit drop in to see me and then drive off, leaving me behind.

When we reached the water, Barry said, "Remember that movie Dad took us to that began with all those guys in track suits running through the waves at the edge of the beach?"

I got the idea. We both pulled off our shoes and socks and began to run up and down the beach, splashing through the little waves that crawled around our feet. The water just about froze our toes. As we ran, I could almost hear the movie sound track.

When we began to pant, we pretended we were running in slow motion the way the movie showed the actors. All the time I

thought about that sad dog waiting for someone who didn't come, maybe was never going
to come. People can be pretty mean sometimes.

Suddenly the dog came racing across the
sand and began to run along with us. We
speeded up, and so did he.

"Good boy, Strider," I said, no longer playing
a part in a movie. I guess I called him Strider
because there is a track club called the Bayside
Striders, and Strider seemed like a good name
for a running dog.

When we reached the shoes and socks we had
left on the beach, Strider shook himself and
slunk, drooping, back to the place by the seawall where we had first seen him. He looked
miserable and guilty.

"Poor old Strider," said Barry. "Something's
sure bothering him." I wasn't surprised when
Barry called the dog Strider. We usually agree.

"Let's take him home," I said as I tried to
wipe the sand from between my toes with my
socks. "Maybe we could find his owner before
the animal control officer gets him."

When we got our shoes and damp socks on
our sandy feet, we called, coaxed, and whistled,
but Strider wouldn't budge. He just looked worried and confused, as if he wanted to follow but
knew he shouldn't. Strider can't talk, but he
sure can act.

The sun was coming out. So were surfers,

who were struggling into wet suits beside their vans. We asked, but no one had ever seen the dog before.

We gave up and walked to my shack because it is closer than Barry's house. Walking in wet sandy socks wasn't much fun.

Oops. Here comes Mom. I'll pretend I'm asleep. I didn't mean to write a novel. More tomorrow.

June 9

Writing all this, I don't feel so lonely at night, and when I am busy, I forget to listen for funny noises.

To continue, Mom still wasn't home from class when Barry and I got back from the beach. We sat on the bathroom floor with our feet in the shower to wash sand from our toes. We didn't say much.

"I bet Strider's hungry," said Barry finally.

"And thirsty," I said.

We raced back to the beach with a couple of hot dogs (sorry, Mom), a bottle of water, and a bowl, feeling as if Strider was going to be hauled off to the gas chamber if we didn't get there in time.

The dog was still there! He slurped water, gulped hot dogs, and looked at us as if we had saved his life. Maybe whatever he has been through is what people mean when they talk about a dog's life.

Barry and I tried to coax Strider to follow us. We didn't touch, we just coaxed. We could tell he was thinking about what he should do, and finally he made a decision. He took a few steps toward us, and a few more, and then he was following us.

Mr. President came along dragging his gunnysacks. "A gentle deed in a naughty world," was all he said.

"What are we going to do with him?" Barry asked on the way back to my place.

"Keep him," I said and remembered how Mom says, "Leigh, always do the right thing," so I added, "just until we phone the SPCA to see if anybody has asked for him."

"Nobody who tells a dog to stay and then leaves him is going to phone the SPCA," said Barry, but admitted I was right.

The lady at the SPCA said no one had inquired about a dog of Strider's description, but wouldn't we like a companion for him? She took our telephone number, just in case, but didn't seem hopeful, which pleased us.

Strider, after sniffing around the shack, flopped down on our thrift-shop rug and slept as if he hadn't slept for a week. Barry and I sat on the couch staring at him. Even if Mom would let me keep Strider until school starts, I knew there was no way I could have him for keeps when we are both away so much. Besides, there was our landlady, Mrs. Smerling, to think of. Mom says I mustn't refer to her as an old bat, even if she is. When we moved in, it seems to me she said something about no pets. We felt lucky she didn't say no boys.

"If nobody claims him, who gets him?" Barry asked the question that had been eating at me.

I really wanted that dog. Wanted him? I needed that dog.

"Would your mom and dad let you keep a dog?" I asked hoping Barry would say no.

Barry shrugged. "We've got everything else running around the house, and we're out of dogs right now."

Strider twitched in his sleep. Sliding off the couch, I petted him gently. I didn't care if that dog barked, bit, chewed up slippers, or chased cats, I loved him and somehow I had to keep him.

"Hey!" said Barry so suddenly that Strider opened his eyes and lifted his head.

"It's all right, boy," I said. He relaxed.

"We could have joint custody," said Barry. "You keep him nights, we both have him days, and when school starts, we can leave him at our house because we have a fenced yard. After school, he would belong to both of us."

"And we can split the cost of dog support!" I was getting excited. "But what about when you go down to Los Angeles to visit your real mom?"

Barry made a face because he likes living with his dad and Mrs. Brinkerhoff more than he likes visiting his real mother. He said, "He'll be all yours for a month, but you could still park him in our yard when you can't be with him. My folks wouldn't care."

Here comes Mom. This is one night I'm not going to pretend to be asleep.

June 10

When Mom opened the door, I held my breath
while she looked at Strider, who raised his
head and wagged his stub of tail.

. "Who have we here?" She looked tired, but
she smiled a half-smile. "A Queensland heeler,
I see. Part wild Australian dingo and part
shepherd. I used to watch them working cattle
when I was a little girl. Good ranch dogs."

The trouble, I could see, was we didn't have
a ranch or a herd of cattle. "His name is
Strider," I said. "Barry and I have joint custody
of him." Then I explained what had happened
and what we planned to do.

Mom smiled a whole smile, but I could see
she was thinking. "Leigh," she said seriously,
"no apartment would let us keep a part-time
dog, and heelers are strong, active dogs. Which

shall it be? A better place to live if we can find
one, or a part-time dog?"

This was a hard question. I wanted half of
Strider (since I couldn't have all of Strider)
more than anything in the world, but it wasn't
fair to have Mom sleep on a couch in the living
room forever. On the other hand, so far no one
with an apartment we can afford has been willing to rent to someone with a boy my age.
When Mom applies, they say they will call
back, but they never do. Apartment managers
seem to expect all boys to write graffiti on the
walls, push drugs, or start rock bands. Finally
I said to Mom, "I'll sleep on the couch."

"Oh well, I'm used to it," she said, "and I
don't want to wake you up when I come in late.
You need a companion evenings while I'm at
work. Yes, you may have joint custody if you
boys can work it out and Mrs. Smerling doesn't
object."

"Mom!" I was horrified. "You don't expect me
to ask her, do you?"

Mom said, "Let's just wait and see what happens. And remember, Leigh, you must always
keep your dog on a leash. A quick, strong dog
like Strider could easily knock someone down."

I vowed his leash would never leave our
hands when we were on the street.

I have a really great mom. Now all I have
to worry about is our landlady. Oh well, Mrs.

Smerling has put up with having me around for a couple of years, so maybe she won't object to a half-time dog.

On the other hand, she might use Strider as an excuse for raising our rent—if she lets him stay.

June 11

Barry's parents said the same thing about our having joint custody of Strider. "If you boys can work it out." Why do grownups think kids can't figure things out? I wonder if Dad would say the same thing. He hasn't been around for a long time.

Barry had a collar and leash left over from some old dog. We split the cost of Strider's license and shots. (There went a lot of floor mopping.) The vet said he was about three years old and in good shape. We decided Barry would hold Strider's leash whenever we came near my place so Mrs. Smerling would think he was Strider's owner.

I have learned one thing about our dog. We can never tell him to sit or stay. If we do, he practically goes to pieces. He gets down on his belly and crawls toward us, whimpering as if to say, "Please don't make me obey those words." Otherwise, he is a good, well-trained dog. I wonder how his former owner felt about giving him up. For some reason he must not have been able to keep him any longer and hoped someone would adopt him.

June 16

For a whole week now, Barry and I have had fun with high-energy Strider. We began by walking him. "Heel," I ordered to see if he would obey. He did, but he nipped our heels to make us go faster. We began to jog. He nipped again, so we began to run. We ran along Ocean View Boulevard where the pinky-purple flowers that cover the ground are so bright they almost hurt our eyes. Below, little waves nibbled at the rocks. Strider gained on us until his leash was almost pulling my arm out of its socket.

Finally we stopped to pant beside a faucet where people wash sand off their feet. "Maybe Strider's pretending we're a herd of cattle," said Barry when he could talk again. Strider caught a drink of water by turning his head sideways under the faucet.

Mr. President came driving his bread truck down the boulevard. He drew up beside us and called out, "So you saved the dog from the vile blows and buffets of the world, to say nothing of the animal control officer."

"We have joint custody!" I called back.

"May fortune smile on your agreement!" Mr. President called out and then drove on.

"I guess that's a fancy way of saying 'If you can work it out.'" Barry sounded cross.

When we returned to our shack, Mrs. Smerling was sitting on her front steps drinking a beer out of an aluminum can. Barry, who quickly took Strider's leash, was full of advice: "If you ask (pant) if you can keep a dog (pant), she'll say no. (Pant pant.) It's easy to say no. (Pant.) Act as if (pant) you're sure a dog (pant)

is okay with her (pant pant) in case she asks questions."

I said, "Hi, Mrs. Smerling (pant pant)," as we approached her. Strider lifted his leg to mark his territory. Barry took hold of Strider's collar as if our dog were his, one hundred percent. This was the smart thing to do, but somehow it made me uncomfortable.

Mrs. Smerling took a swig from the can before she said, "Hello there, Leigh. I see you have a couple of friends."

"That's right, Mrs. Smerling," I said as we walked past her.

It is hard to tell when our landlady is being nice. At least she isn't fussy about Strider lifting his leg on her shrubbery because she never prunes or waters it. However, on the first of the month, at 8 A.M. sharp, she comes down the path in her bathrobe with her thong sandals flapping and calls out, "Mrs. Botts! Mrs. Botts!" As soon as Mom opens the door, she says, "Your rent is due," as if she suspects we can't pay it. Mom dreads the first of the month because the old—oops!—Mrs. Smerling might raise our rent, which is already high.

Inside, Barry and I flopped down on the couch. We were hot and sweaty, but we felt great. A running dog is a great dog to own. I mean half-own.

Strider went to his water dish and slurped. Then he rolled over on his back, which meant he trusted us. We both scratched his belly. Being trusted by a dog, especially a dog that has good reason for not trusting humans, is a nice feeling.

June 22

Time goes fast these days. Barry and I begin each morning by running with Strider. On the mornings I mop for Katy, Barry holds Strider's leash and waits for me. Katy says we have an interesting custody arrangement if we can make it work, and she gives us samples of whatever she is preparing for a party. Strider enjoys chicken livers wrapped in bacon.

One day after our run, when I was reading and Barry was pretending to order expensive camping gear from catalogs, he ran across something called a "dog posture dish." The catalog explained the importance of a dog's skeletal alignment and showed a picture of a dog standing up eating from dishes set on a platform so the dog didn't have to bend down.

Barry and I thought this was funny. "Strider,

old boy, how's your skeletal alignment?" I asked. Strider, who has a straight, strong back, looked interested.

"You know, that's not a bad idea," said Barry. "Let's go up to my place and build him a posture dish out of Dad's scrap lumber." We fastened Strider's leash to his collar and raced up the hill, where we sawed and hammered until we produced a workable stand for Strider's dishes. I lugged it down the hill, and now Strider seems pleased to eat standing up with his spine aligned.

Another day when I was reading and Barry was studying his catalogs, Strider, looking bored, wandered around the shack.

"Too bad he can't read, too," Barry remarked.

"Great idea," I said. "Let's teach him."

Barry was doubtful, but I reasoned that if Strider could read words he didn't like to hear, he might not get so upset when we told him to sit or stay. I printed SIT on one piece of paper and STAY on another, and we went to work. We held up SIT and pushed down on Strider's hindquarters to make him sit. It took a while, but he finally caught on. STAY was harder. Barry held up the card. I went into the kitchen. Strider followed because that is where I feed him. I led him back. We went through the whole thing again until finally, after a couple of days, Strider caught on or gave in, I'm not sure which. Now I carry two pieces of paper with the magic words in my hip pocket whenever I take Strider out. They might come in handy.

Mom thinks teaching a dog to read is funny. Maybe it is, but Barry and I had a lot of fun doing it. Maybe someday I could run a school for teaching dogs to read. (Joke.) Too bad Boyd Henshaw didn't think of this when he wrote *Ways to Amuse a Dog*, which used to be my favorite book.

June 30

Tomorrow Barry has to fly down to what he calls Los Smogland with two of his little sisters to visit their real mother and stepfather. He will be gone for a month, so I was invited over for a farewell dinner.

Mr. Brinkerhoff, who works in heavy construction—highways and stuff like that—came home and said, "Glad to see you, Leigh. With so many women around, us men have to stick together." That made me feel good. He also invited Strider into the house, which made me, but not the girls' cats, feel even better. I showed the little sisters how Strider could read. They were impressed by his intelligence and printed ROLL OVER on a paper, but he ignored them. The oldest girl said he had a reading problem.

The part of the Brinkerhoff house I like best is the spaghetti wall. To see if the spaghetti is cooked enough, the family take turns throwing a strand at a wall in the kitchen. If the spaghetti sticks, it is done; if it slides to the floor, it needs to cook longer. When enough spaghetti has stuck to the wall, they spray-paint over it and start again. The wall reminds me of modern art I have seen in books at the library.

The Brinkerhoffs invited me to take a turn. My strand stuck! I know it is silly, but having my spaghetti stick to the wall made me feel good, as if I had accomplished something really important. Maybe that's what my future should be—throwing spaghetti for one of those plants that freezes Italian dinners for supermarkets.

We all sat down at the big round table to a meal of spaghetti and meatballs and a huge bowl of green salad full of avocado, cheese, and bits of salami. The littlest girl sat in a high chair and ate with her fingers and smeared tomato sauce all over her face and in her hair. Things like that don't bother Mrs. Brinkerhoff. Sometimes I wish Mom were more like Mrs. Brinkerhoff. Not all the time, just once in a while.

The girls told stupid riddles and screamed with laughter while Barry and I exchanged looks that said we were too grown-up for such childish jokes. Mr. Brinkerhoff gave Strider a meatball which he gulped down. I slipped him another. Mom doesn't allow me to feed Strider at the table when she's home.

I was sorry when it was time to leave. "So long, Barry," I said as I snapped Strider's leash in place. We were outside, standing by the fence. "Have fun down there in Los Smogland."

"Yeah." Barry sounded gloomy. "So long, and good luck in hiding Strider from Mrs. Smerling." He stroked Strider's ears as if he didn't want to part with him.

I thought, Strider is in my custody for a whole month. Not joint custody. *My* custody.

July 8

Strider has been mine for a whole week! I brush him, wrestle with him, and we run a lot to avoid Mrs. Smerling. I always wave to Mr. President when I see him, and think of the day Barry and I found an abandoned dog. We run a little farther each day. Now we go around the Point, where I can take Strider off his leash and where we can hear sea lions bark. Strider, who rarely barks, enjoys barking at sea lions.

On foggy mornings we have to time our run around the Point to avoid the blast of the foghorn. Once it caught us and nearly blew us off the road. I could actually feel the sound waves. Strider took off at top speed. I thought he was gone for good, but I finally found him behind a rock. He must remember because he always speeds up as we pass the foghorn, even if the sun is shining.

One day, when we were cooling down along the beach, I found a perfectly good golf ball. When I poked around the kelp that had washed up, I found another. After that I picked up a golf ball or two every day, washed them, packed them in egg cartons, and sold them at one of the pro shops. I thought I had a second source of income.

Then Strider caught on and began to hunt for golf balls with me. He even jumped into a water hazard on the P.G. golf course to retrieve them. When he found one, he carried it in his mouth and dropped it at my feet. Then he looked up at me and waggled, not just his tail stub, but all over, he was so eager for praise. I hugged him, and he licked my face with his slippery tongue.

Then something funny (to me) happened. We were running past a rich people's golf course when Strider spotted a golf ball on the fairway. He shot off, grabbed the ball, and dropped it at my feet. Four golfers riding on two carts began to shout and wave their clubs at us. Then they began to pursue us on their carts. I threw the ball back onto the fairway and fled with Strider.

When we were safe, I stopped and laughed because the whole thing was so much like a comedy on TV. Strider always looks pleased when I laugh. Sometimes I think Strider, not Barry, is my best friend. I'll be glad to see Barry again, but I'll be sorry—oh well, I can't have everything. Half a dog is better than none, as the saying goes.

Strider has a new habit. Whenever we stop, he places his paw on my foot. It isn't an accident because he always does it. I like to think he doesn't want to leave me.

July 9

Today when I took Strider out, the fog was beginning to lift. The sun felt so good I sat on a bench at the Point to enjoy it. Strider lay with his nose on my foot. The morning was so peaceful I sat with my eyes closed, listening to the *skree* of gulls, waves whispering around rocks, bees humming on flowers, and crunching of joggers' feet on the path. I am not sure what I thought about—Mom studying hard, Dad off in his rig someplace with a load of turnips, Barry cooped up in an apartment in Los Smogland? I really don't know.

When Strider woke up, we ran some more. I saw Mr. President picking up trash, but Strider never wants to stop at that part of the beach. We ran past the high school where I will go in September. The playing field looks like a good place to run, but a sign says, "Dogs not allowed on infield or track."

That's the way our days have gone, with a few detours to the laundromat and the library. So far, Strider and I have avoided Mrs. Smerling.

July 10

I spoke too soon. Today when Strider and I came running home, Mrs. Smerling, wearing an old bathrobe, stepped out of her back door with a broom in her hand. Funny, she doesn't sweep the steps that often. Was she spying? We had to stop. Mrs. Smerling watched Strider mark his territory, which he has done so often he probably thinks he owns the place.

"Whose dog is that, anyway?" she asked. When I explained about joint custody, she said, "I see," as if she didn't.

I added, "Barry is visiting his real mother this month because she has joint custody. Of him, I mean."

Mrs. Smerling looked confused.

"He's a good dog," I said. "He's not really a barker. That's because he's part Australian dingo, a breed that doesn't often bark. Sometimes his shepherd blood barks, but not much." I felt silly. Blood doesn't bark, as a teacher would say. Dogs bark.

Strider sat down, paw on my foot, ears up, and acted the part of a good dog while I stood there trying to look responsible and wondering if a barking watchdog approach might have been better. "I keep him outdoors as much as possible," was all I could think to say.

"So I notice." Mrs. Smerling went on sweeping her back steps.

So she's been watching us all the time, but where do we stand? It might help if Strider chased off a burglar or did something brave.

July 13

Today the mailman brought a postcard from Barry with a picture of Disneyland and a note that said, "There's nothing much to do down here but watch TV and keep my sisters from falling into the swimming pool. How's Strider? Does he miss me?"

I wondered. Maybe Strider has forgotten Barry.

July 18

Something happened today! Dad turned up, live and in person. Strider and I had come home from an early afternoon run, and there he was, sitting in his tractor, waiting. When he saw me, he climbed down from his cab and hugged me. His stomach isn't as hard as it used to be. Bandit was watching. I noticed that although Dad had a dusty look, and so did his tractor, which he used to keep shining, Bandit was wearing a clean red bandana around his neck. Dad has always been good about that.

Dad looked me over. "You're shooting—" he began, and changed to, "You're growing like a weed." He didn't say "shooting up" because that sounds like drugs. Maybe he worries about drugs like Mom does.

Then he said, "But you're going to have to put on muscle if you expect to play football."

I don't expect to play football. I don't even *want* to play football, even if he was a big high school football star.

I must have frowned because he looked at Strider and said, "Who's this?"

When I explained, he let Bandit out of the cab. My ex-dog looked older and fatter. Strider's hair stood up. The two dogs weren't exactly friendly, but they didn't growl, either. After sniffing around, ears up, tail wagging, Bandit marked a bush or two, Dad snapped his fingers, Bandit jumped into the cab, and that was that. I doubt if he remembered me. Maybe Strider has forgotten Barry.

Dad and I, with Strider nipping along, went into our shack. We had trouble talking, so we sat staring at a stupid game show until Mom came in. I was embarrassed because Mom caught us watching a man and a woman jumping up and down, screaming, and hugging the master of ceremonies because they had won a dishwasher and a set of luggage. I snapped off the TV.

Dad got up and kissed Mom, a just-friends kiss, not a madly-in-love kiss. At least they get along without fighting. Barry's dad and real mom quarrel over the telephone, which makes Barry unhappy.

Dad said, "I was in this area, so I thought I would drop off the support check in person."

"Thanks, Bill." Mom took the check, but she didn't tell him she deposits as much as she can in the bank for my college education. Support stops when I am eighteen.

"How about me taking you two out to eat?" Dad asked. We went out for a late lunch before Mom had to leave for the hospital. Dad and I had burritos and Mom had a taco salad.

We looked like a real family, so I pretended we were. Then I began to worry. There are no crops in P.G., unless you count tourists. How come Dad didn't have a load? A trucker without a load is losing money. I didn't ask questions because I didn't want to spoil being a family.

Afterward, as Dad drove off, I couldn't help thinking that a tractor that isn't pulling a load is like a lizard that has lost its tail. It can go fast, but there should be more to it.

July 20

Today Mom said I had to take our washing to
the laundromat, which usually makes me mad,
but this time I was still feeling good from Dad's
visit, so I didn't complain. When I got there, I
hitched Strider to a light post and held up the
STAY sign. Then I loaded the washer by the
window so he wouldn't feel abandoned and
worked as fast as I could before any kids from
school came along and saw me.

After that I went next door to the thrift
shop to look for a thin paperback to stuff in
my back pocket so I would have something to
read whenever Strider and I stopped to rest.
I was paying for *The Human Comedy,* by Wil-
liam Saroyan, when I saw a shirt hanging on
a rack of clothes. It was a brand-new shirt
my size, a shirt with imagination, a shirt that

shouted, "Buy me! Take me out of here!" I really liked that shirt, but I felt I wasn't the type. If I wore such a wild shirt, everyone would laugh.

Back in the laundromat, I moved the clothes from the washer to the dryer as fast as I could. Outside, I sat on the curb with my feet in the gutter, opened *The Human Comedy,* and began to read about a boy in Fresno.

Wouldn't you know? A girl with long wavy red hair came along on her bike. I had seen her—Jessica or Jennifer or something that begins with a *J*—around school because nobody can miss a girl with hair like that. She stopped in front of me and said, "Leigh Botts, what are you doing there with your feet in the gutter?"

"Reading." I didn't know what else to say.

"That's what I thought," she said and pedaled away with her long hair flying.

I sat there feeling silly for a minute. Then suddenly I felt great. Dad had come to see us, I had grown, and a *girl* knew my name. I felt so great I went into the thrift shop and bought that shirt.

"Wear it in good health!" the thrift shop lady called after me.

At home I put on the shirt and looked in the bathroom mirror, the only mirror we have. The shirt looked as good as I thought it would. The left side is blue with pink dots, and the left

sleeve is pink with blue dots. The right side is
purple with blue crosswise stripes, and the
right sleeve is blue with pink dots. I twisted
around so I could see the back. One half is purple and blue crosswise stripes, and the other is
green and blue up-and-down stripes. The collar
and cuffs are plain purple. The best part is I

chose it myself and paid for it with money I had earned. I felt as good as my shirt looked.

I heard Mom come in, so I burst out of the bathroom. "Ta-da! Like it?" I asked. "I bought it for school."

"Well—it will take a little getting used to, but I'm glad you have the courage to wear it." Mom looked so pleased I was surprised.

Then I got to thinking. Mom looked that way because I never would have worn such a shirt when I was a new kid in school moping around, being miserable about the divorce, and trying to look inconspicuous.

I hung my shirt in my closet to keep it new for school, put on an old T-shirt, and took Strider for a run. My feet felt so light they skimmed the path by the bay. A great shirt and a girl who knew my name. On a scale of one to ten, I would rate this a ten day.

July 30

Yesterday Mr. Brinkerhoff invited Strider and
me to go to the airport to meet Barry's plane.
We had to wait outside because dogs are not
allowed in airports. When the plane landed and
Barry saw his father, he let go of his sisters'
hands and threw his arms around Mr. Brinkerhoff as if he never wanted to let go. His father
hugged him just as hard. When they parted
and looked at each other, Barry had tears in
his eyes but managed to say, "Dad, it sure is
good to be back."

I had tears in my eyes, too, because my dad
and I hug, but not like that.

Barry grinned and said, "Hi, Leigh." Then,
to hide his feelings he said, "Hello there,
Strider, old boy. How's our dog?"

Strider wagged his piece of tail and sat down

with his chin up and ears back, which meant he wanted to be petted.

I tensed up, waiting to see if Strider would place his paw on Barry's foot. He kept all four feet on the sidewalk.

Whew!

August 10

Now that Barry has returned, summer is going fast. Barry puffs when we run with Strider. After being exercised by my, I mean *our,* dog for the past month, I don't puff at all.

When I showed Barry my shirt, he fell over on the couch laughing and said, "You mean you're going to wear *that* to school?"

"Sure," I said. "You're just jealous."

"Me, jealous? Of *that*?" Barry laughed some more. I started to pound him, and we scuffled. This made Strider so anxious we stopped. We weren't sure which of us he would defend, but I was pretty sure it was me. I mean I.

I wish I could forget Barry's saying, "Me, jealous?"

August 19

Last night Dad telephoned from Bakersfield to say that today he was coming through Salinas with a load of garlic and wanted to know if I would meet him at the bus station and ride with him to the dehydrator in Gilroy. Would I!

I got up early this morning, whizzed around with the mop at Catering by Katy, exercised Strider, showered, left Strider in Barry's yard, and caught the bus to Salinas. A couple of minutes after I got there, Dad came barreling up in his tractor. He was hauling two flatbed trailers loaded with wooden bins of garlic stacked two high and tied on with cables.

I climbed into the cab beside Dad, who asked, "How're you doing, Leigh?" Bandit looked up from his bunk behind the seat and went back to sleep.

I told Dad I was doing okay, and we drove off smelling of garlic. An empty Styrofoam cup rolled around the floor of the cab.

Traffic was heavy on 101. There were tractors hauling double gondolas of tomatoes or grapes, and because summer vacation is almost over, tourists with carloads of kids were hurrying toward home.

High in the cab, I had a good view of the Santa Clara Valley. We passed acres of tomatoes,

cauliflower, and spinach, a few dying orchards,
and beautiful fields of flowers. Zinnias, I think
they are called, and marigolds. I asked Dad if
the people who raised them got the idea from
the Steinbeck story of the man who raised acres
of sweet peas. Or maybe it was the other way
around. John Steinbeck got the idea for his story
from fields like these. Dad said he wouldn't
know, but he did know the flowers were raised
for seed, which brought a good price.

Because of the dehydrator, Gilroy is a town you can smell before you see it. Once before when I rode with Dad, the whole town smelled like frying onions, which made me hungry for a hamburger. Today, when the dehydrator was working garlic, Gilroy smelled like Mrs. Brinkerhoff's kitchen when she makes spaghetti sauce.

As we turned off near the dehydrator, the air was so heavy with the smell of garlic that it made my mouth water. "Do you suppose the garlic smell makes everybody in Gilroy salivate all the time?" I asked. *Salivate.* That's a word I had never used before. I usually say drool, but salivate is a good word to save for school. Teachers like large vocabularies.

"Nah," said Dad. "They're so used to it they probably can't even smell it."

After the garlic was unloaded at the dehydrator, we were so hungry from the smell of garlic that we stopped for pizza for us and water for Bandit. As Dad and I sat facing each other under a wall-mounted TV set showing reruns of boxing matches, Dad asked, "Leigh, you made any plans for the future?" He spoke through a mouthful of pizza. Dad always eats fast. In places like this, he also eats with his cap on. He wouldn't if Mom were around.

"Oh, not really," I admitted. The future is something I try not to worry about.

"Just don't drive a truck like your old man," Dad told me. "It's a rough life. Sleeping in the cab and eating in cafés gets old after a few years."

"I wasn't planning to," I said. Now that I took a good look at Dad, he did look tired. Maybe all those country-western songs about truckers are true.

Suddenly Dad asked, "How's your mother getting along?"

"Okay," I said. "She works pretty hard."

"She making any friends?" he asked.

What Dad really wanted to know was, Does she have any *men* friends? Dad had let me ride with him so he could snoop. This made me so mad I said, "Sure she has friends. They get together to make stuffed animals to sell at craft fairs." I wasn't going to squeal on Mom and tell him about Bob from the hospital lab, who sometimes jogs with her and stops by for breakfast, or the paramedic who drives an ambulance, wears a beeper, and takes both of us out to dinner once in a while. Mom always refers to him as the Beeper. Nice guys, both of them, but I don't think Mom is serious.

Dad was silent, trying to think how he could find out what he wanted to know without letting me know what it was he wanted to know. I was so annoyed I asked, "What about you, Dad? Are you making any friends?"

Dad shot me a look that wasn't exactly friendly. "Sure," he said. "I got lots of friends."

We let it go at that. I didn't really want to know about the friends Dad makes at truck stops. As we sat facing one another in that booth, it seemed to me that Dad and I didn't have much to say to each other. Maybe we never did.

Dad made good time back to the Salinas bus stop, but we were quiet most of the way. Without a load, Dad was losing money and was in a hurry to get to Bakersfield to load up more bins of garlic. As I watched him drive off, I felt sad. If he asks questions about Mom, he must be lonely, deep down. I wish I had been nicer.

August 20

My pants are too short! All of them!

When Mom and I were looking over my clothes for school, I got out my pants and discovered they don't even reach my ankles. They are only good for cutoffs, which are what I have been wearing all summer. I wondered if Mom had noticed the hair I was growing on my legs.

Mom hugged me and said, "I'm going to miss my little boy." Then we were off to Penney's for pants. We left Strider shut in the shack.

After pants, we went to the shirt department, where I reminded Mom of my thrift shop shirt which I was saving for school.

She said, "Oh, that shirt," as if she was both amused and annoyed by it.

As we drove home, I couldn't forget her remark about missing her little boy. It made me feel guilty. How am I supposed to become a man and be her little boy at the same time?

There was nothing I could do about it, I decided. Besides, I have new pants, hair on my legs, and a great shirt.

By the time we came home, Strider had eaten a corner out of the rug. It's a good thing it's our rug, not Mrs. Smerling's.

September 12

Today I discovered two kinds of people go to high school: those who wear new clothes to show off on the first day, and those who wear their oldest clothes to show they think school is unimportant.

This morning I ran with Strider, mopped Katy's floor, ran home to shower, and put on my shirt. Then I hurried up to the Brinkerhoffs' to leave Strider in their yard.

Barry was waiting. "You're brave," he said when he saw my shirt.

At the intersection near school we met a boy a little taller than I named Kevin Knight, who was new in junior high last semester. He's a rich kid. Anyone can tell by his expensive watch, ironed sport shirts, and chinos with creases instead of jeans. Even his haircuts look expensive.

Kevin scowled at me. "That's my shirt you're wearing," he informed me.

"It can't be," I said. "I bought it at the thrift shop." Then I wished I hadn't mentioned the thrift shop to this rich kid.

"It was my favorite shirt," said Kevin, "but my mother hated it so much she gave it to the thrift shop before I even had a chance to wear it."

Some mom. "Why did she have to do that?" I asked, understanding how a new shirt happened to be in the thrift shop.

"She said it was in appalling taste." Kevin looked angry, and I didn't blame him.

"Too bad, Kevin," I said. "It's my shirt now. I paid for it."

"Gimme my shirt," said Kevin and made a grab for it.

I dodged. Kevin grabbed again. I wasn't going to lose that shirt, so I ducked and began to run with Kevin chasing me. Our book bags thumped our backs. I reached the school grounds one step ahead of him, ducked, dodged, twisted out of his grasp, and ran some more.

Kids began to yell, "You in the fancy shirt— go!" "Come on, Leigh!" "Get him, Kevin!" "Leigh, go!" I was surprised that so many people knew my name.

I had to stay ahead or lose my shirt in front of the whole school. Pounding down the breezeway past the classroom doors, I looked back to see how close Kevin was and bumped into a teacher who held me by the arm. Maybe he was the principal. "You know the saying, my lad," he said. "Never look back. Someone might be gaining on you."

Kevin, panting, caught up. "You better (pant) watch out," he gasped. "I'll (pant) get my shirt (pant) back yet."

I couldn't resist taunting, "What for? (Pant.) Your mother won't let you wear it." That was mean, and I knew it.

"Some shirt," said the teacher.

The chase was over for today. But tomorrow?

My teachers seem okay, but I'm not sure about my English teacher, Ms. Habis-Jones, who looks unhappy and wears her hair twisted into a knob on top of her head. She ties a white scarf around the knob, which makes her hair look as if it had been wounded and bandaged. When she said that in her classroom we would write, write, write, the guy behind me whispered, "Rah, rah, rah!" She says she will not tolerate non-words such as gonna, kinda, and sorta.

In gym I discovered I am no longer the mediumest boy in my class. I thought if my pants were too short, every other guy's pants would be too short, too, but it hasn't worked out that way. When we lined up according to height in gym, I was toward the tall end of the line. Why do we have to line up according to height anyway? Do teachers think we look neater that way? If we lined up according to width, I would be near the front of the line because I am skinny.

September 16

After that first day, I washed my shirt every night, hung it in the shower, smoothed it while it was damp, and put it on again the next morning. Kevin waits every morning, but I keep ahead of him, and we both outrun Barry. Kevin's legs are longer, but I have more stamina, thanks to Strider. Sometimes he gets close enough to grab my shirt. Then I turn and chase him for a change. It wasn't long before half the school was watching and cheering. The red-headed girl cheered, too, but she yelled, "Come on, Joseph!" She has forgotten my name, or maybe she means Kevin. Her name is Geneva Weston. I found that out by what are called "discreet inquiries."

One morning a man who must be the fittest teacher in the school grabbed us both by the

arms and said, "I'd like to see you boys harness that energy and turn out for cross-country now and track next spring." I found out later he was Mr. Kurtz, the track coach. Not being the football type like Barry, I hadn't thought much about sports before. Running makes me feel good, but I don't like to run where I can trip in gopher holes, so I don't think I'll go out for cross-country.

September 19

This morning Mom said, "*Please,* Leigh, wear a different shirt today."

"Why?" I asked. "What's wrong with this one?" I don't like Mom telling me what to do. I'm not a little kid anymore. My pants proved that.

"No real reason," she said. "Just a change of scene."

Since she wasn't giving me a direct order, I decided to go along with her. Besides, I don't want to wear out my shirt. It is valuable because it stands for my not being a wimp.

When Barry and I met Kevin, he demanded, "Where's my shirt?"

"In my closet," I told him. Out of habit, we began to run, not really chasing, just running. Barry was able to keep up, which was good. I hadn't liked leaving Barry behind while I defended my honor.

At school, kids began to tease me: "Hey, look! Leigh has a clean shirt." This didn't bother me. I know my shirt is always clean.

When I was about to enter my math room, the redheaded girl came down the breezeway. "Hi, Joseph," she said. "What happened to your coat of many colors?"

Geneva hadn't forgotten my name. She was referring to the Bible story about Joseph and his coat of many colors I learned about in Sunday school when we lived in Bakersfield.

"My shirt needs a rest," I told her and ducked into my classroom because I didn't know what else to say. I didn't learn much math because I thought about the girl instead of algebra equations. Her hair isn't really red, and calling her carrot-top would be inaccurate. I tried to think of the right word. Rust? Orange? Chestnut? Copper? None seemed right.

After class Mr. Gray, who seems to have years of chalk dust ground into him, stopped me and said, "Leigh, you'd better stop daydreaming and pay attention in class." He was right. Mom said if my grades dropped, the TV set would have to go.

September 21

~~Lots of~~ Many things have happened lately. (I guess you can call that a topic sentence. My English teacher is enthusiastic about topic sentences.) The most important ~~thing~~ event ~~happened~~ last night, which was Mom's night off. We were watching the Olympics on TV when the phone rang. I answered because I was closest. To my surprise, Dad was on the line. For a second I thought about how I used to long for Dad to call, and now I was thinking about how great athletes from all over the world looked marching into the stadium. "Oh, hi, Dad," I said. "Where are you?"

"In Cholame." He sounded worried. "Is your mother there?"

Mom took the telephone. "Hi, Bill," she said. "This is a surprise."

. While she listened, I wondered why Dad was worrying in Cholame, which is just a wide place in the road in a dusty valley between Highways 101 and 5.

Finally Mom said, "I'm sorry, Bill. Really sorry."

I ran my hand over Strider's rough hair and wondered what she was sorry about. She soon told me. The transmission of Dad's tractor had broken down. He was waiting for a tow truck to tow him into Paso Robles, where he will have to wait for a new transmission to be sent up from L.A. First he had to wait for another tractor to haul his load of tomatoes to the soup plant. Even though tomatoes are grown for a long shelf life, they rot fast in the sun.

"A transmission means big bucks," I told Mom. "And if those tomatoes don't reach the loading dock on schedule, Dad is in money trouble."

"Don't I know it?" said Mom. "And the tractor isn't even paid for. Your father took out a six-year loan to buy it, and if he gets more than two months behind in payments, the bank will take it." She sounded so sad and so discouraged I didn't know what to say, so I slid down on the floor and hugged Strider, who laid his nose against my neck. I continued to watch the Olympics, but my thoughts were in Cholame.

September 24

Mom and I haven't been getting along as well as we used to. Maybe we are both worried about Dad, or maybe this shack is so small we are getting in each other's hair. Even though I outgrew my pants, she forgets I'm not a little kid any longer. She is always after me about something, especially about taking our washing to the laundromat, a job I *hate* and postpone until our laundry practically ferments. She says doing what is expected of me without complaining is a sign of maturity. Yeah, yeah. What about longer pants as a sign of maturity?

If some landlord ever had an attack of kindness and rented us a two-bedroom apartment, it might have a laundry room in the basement, where the whole world couldn't see me with our washing.

I admire Mom, even when she's mad at me, and I know she loves me. I'm not so sure about Dad, who never gets mad at me. Maybe he doesn't care enough. We haven't heard from him since he called about his breakdown. I picture him sitting alone on a dusty road beside a double trailer-load of tomatoes beginning to smell like old catsup.

September 26

Today was a real shocker. This evening, while Mom was at work and I was studying, Dad telephoned with more news. He has lost his rig! After he had the tractor transmission replaced, he had to admit he couldn't pay for it until after the tomato season and that he was a month behind in his payments to the bank. The repair people kept the keys, settled with the bank, and now they have the tractor and Dad doesn't. Boom! Just like that.

Now all Dad has to drive is a beat-up pickup truck.

He towed his house-trailer he had used as home base from Bakersfield to Salinas, where he has a temporary job pumping gas until something better turns up. He said he wanted to be closer to us, something I never expected to hear him say. Nothing was said about support payments, and it wasn't the time to ask. He sounded so discouraged and sort of ashamed that I feel terrible.

Dad without his rig! The first time I saw him drive it, I thought he was the biggest, strongest man in the world, and nothing could ever happen to him.

September 30

In English we finished studying *The Rime of the Ancient Mariner,* about an old sailor who corners a wedding guest and makes him listen to a long story about shooting an albatross, thereby placing a curse on his ship. It was a pretty good poem except Ms. Habis-Jones made us pick it to pieces.

Today she said, "Now we are going to write, write, write."

The boy behind me whispered, "Rah, rah, rah." She glared.

At first I thought she was going to make us write essays on such topics as the mariner's motivation in shooting the albatross. Maybe she doesn't really like the poem because, instead of some bird-related treatise, she told us to write a paragraph on any subject and to pay special attention to the topic sentence.

I thought about *The Rime of the Ancient Mariner* being written as if the old sailor were telling it. I also thought about gonna and sorta and all the words Ms. Habis-Jones said were not acceptable in her classroom. This made me want to use them. There is something about Ms. Habis-Jones that makes me feel ornery. Since Dad lost his rig, I feel ornery to the nth degree, as we say in algebra, about almost anything.

I wrote, "The old man said to the stranger, 'I gotcha cornered, and I'm gonna tell ya about my dog. Ya gotta listen even if ya don't wanna. My dog's coat is sorta rough, but his ears are kinda soft. He knows howta heel. His eyes say, Gimme your attention, gimme your love, gimme a bone. Whatcha think of that? When I walk him, he always hasta lift his leg. Ya oughta see my dog.' The stranger said, 'Lemme go. I don't care aboucher dog.'"

I had fun writing the paragraph and thought it had a good topic sentence.

Ms. Habis-Jones, who was patrolling the aisles like a guard, stopped at my desk to read over my shoulder. Then she picked up my paper and read it to the class, who laughed. She asked, "Class, what is wrong with this paragraph?"

One of those generic goody-goody girls raised

her hand. "Leigh used improper words such as gonna and sorta."

"That is correct," said old Wounded-hair, who always speaks in complete sentences. "Leigh, what words should you have used?"

I tried to argue. "My paragraph is spoken. The people speak that way, so the words I used are correct."

Ms. Wounded-hair dropped my paper on my desk and said, "At the beginning of the semester I said I would not tolerate improper words in this classroom. Rewrite your paper correctly."

"But that will make it incorrect," I said, still trying to argue. "I was writing about people who don't speak correctly."

Ms. Wounded-hair looked annoyed. "Leigh, you need to improve your attitude," she informed me. I suppose she has the right to lay down rules for her class. She loves rules. The more the better. She would probably tell Samuel Taylor Coleridge to improve his attitude because he had his Ancient Mariner speak words like o'ertaking and ne'er, but I didn't say so. You can't argue with some teachers. If she were grading his poem, she would put a red check over *Rime* because he didn't spell it *Rhyme*. Then she would mark his paper C—.

October 4

I still feel so cross with old Wounded-hair (today her scarf was white with pink dots, which made it look as if it had been peppered with bird shot) that I feel cross with other people, too, even Barry, because he has gone out for football, a sport that doesn't interest me. I mean playing. I enjoy watching. After school I collect Strider alone and go watch the frosh-soph team practice. Barry feels so tired and sore he doesn't feel like running anymore. He leaves Strider to me.

Today, when Strider and I came to the apartment house in front of our shack, I began, as usual, to look around to see where Mrs. Smerling was so we could sneak in without her seeing us. Wouldn't you know? There she was, with her hair hanging down in a braid, going through the trash, trying to jam it all down into two cans so she won't have to pay for three cans, one for each of the two apartments and one for our cottage.

"Hello there, Leigh," she said as she stomped on a carton.

"Good afternoon, Mrs. Smerling," I said. Politeness often pays. Strider lifted his leg on a dusty geranium.

"How's school?" she asked. Adults always ask that. They don't really care.

"About three on a scale of one to ten." I tried to smile, even though my stomach was tied in a knot.

She looked at Strider, who was putting on his good-dog act: ears up, eyes bright, a doggy smile on his face. I hurried him into the shack before she could say anything.

Sometimes I wish she would raise our rent, end our suspense, and put us out of our misery.

November 25

October and November were so boring I didn't
have anything to write in my diary. My attitude isn't great. I am haunted by Dad, who
lives close enough to come to see me but
doesn't. Maybe he is too ashamed because he
lost his rig.

One day Mom said, "Leigh, you really get on
my nerves when you call this place a shack.
This is our home. I am doing the best I can. It
isn't my fault rents are so high and your father
can't keep up his support payments."

I know I looked sulky, but I was really
ashamed. She was right. Everything I do seems
wrong. I worry a lot, mostly about Dad washing windshields after being a trucker.

Things were better yesterday because the
Brinkerhoffs invited Mom and me to Thanks-

giving dinner. Mr. Brinkerhoff cooked the turkey, his specialty, and carved it with a flourish. The grandmother was there, knitting a wild red, purple, and orange sweater out of fluffy yarn, which Mom admired and Barry says will sell for several hundred dollars. The little girls were all flapping around in the monarch butterfly costumes they wore in P.G.'s annual butterfly parade in October. We had all the things that go with turkey, and two kinds of pie. Everyone laughed a lot. Mom laughed, too, and admired the spaghetti wall. It was good to hear her laugh.

After that dinner, our *cottage* seemed small and cold. I fed Strider the scraps Mrs. Brinkerhoff had sent him and wondered where Dad ate his Thanksgiving dinner.

I wish Mom would laugh more often.

December 17

Running with Strider is cold, damp work. I overheard one of the gas station attendants next door say, "Doesn't that kid ever walk?" He ought to try substituting for a herd of cattle to exercise a Queensland heeler.

Old Wounded-hair now gives me A's on my compositions and says my attitude has improved. Ha-ha. That's what she thinks. I hand in the most boring papers I can think of, but I am careful to make them correct. Writing "My Summer at Camp" was especially interesting to write because I have never gone to camp. My topic sentence was "I made many friends at camp." Boring!

I worry about Dad, I worry about Mom, I worry about me. Wiping up Strider's muddy paw prints so Mrs. Smerling won't see them is an ongoing job.

December 25

Christmas! Friday Barry left for Los Smogland
with his two real sisters to spend vacation with
Real Mom. I now have Strider all to myself for
ten days.

This morning Dad turned up in his old
pickup truck to bring me a quilted jacket for
Christmas. He gave me quilted jackets the last
two Christmases, but he forgets. Or maybe he
doesn't know what else to get. I gave him a
warm shirt to wear under his uniform to keep
him warm when he has to go out in the cold
to check oil and wash windshields.

Because Mom had Thanksgiving off, she had
to work today. She cooked us a nice midday
dinner with roast chicken, so she invited Dad
to stay. Nobody objected when I slipped a bite
to Strider. Dad left right after we ate because

he had to work, too. He was pretty quiet the whole time.

"Buck up, Leigh." Mom kissed me as she left for work. I washed the dishes to keep hordes of beady-eyed, antennae-waving cockroaches from invading.

Today is not exactly a Joyeux Noël, as they say on Christmas cards. The good part is I am free of old Wounded-hair for the holidays, and I have Strider all to myself.

January 6

The day before Christmas vacation ended, serious rain came pounding down. Our cottage didn't leak, but the windows steamed, and mildew drew a map on the bathroom wall. One morning I woke up feeling awful and said, "Mom, I have a sore throat and I think I have a temperature."

Mom laid her hand on my forehead and said, "Everybody has a temperature. You have a *fever*." That's what working in the hospital has done to her—made her sound like my English teacher. Being Mom, she began to worry full-time and said she'd better phone the hospital and say she couldn't work that day.

"Mom," I croaked. "I'm not dying. I'm old enough to stay alone. I'm not a baby, and I have Strider to keep me company."

Because the hospital was shorthanded, Mom finally agreed to let me stay alone if I promised to stay in bed, drink lots of fluids, etc., etc. She made me a bed on the living room couch because my room is unheated, took Strider jogging in the rain, and dried him on an old towel so the shack wouldn't smell too doggy; and before she left, she set water, juice, books, and a thermos of hot soup on a chair by the couch.

The rest of the day stretched ahead like a long, dark tunnel. I didn't even feel up to watching TV. Strider and I dozed until he began to act restless. I forced myself to get up and open the door for him. "Hurry up," I ordered because rain was blowing in, and I felt weak. He obliged. Good dog, Strider.

Later, I poured soup but wasn't hungry. I must have dozed, because it was dark when I heard footsteps on the path. They were too heavy to be Mom's. She has light, quick steps. Strider stood up, pricked his ears, raised his hair, dropped his haunches, ready to spring.

I raised up on one elbow until I heard, "Leigh, it's Dad."

"Down, boy," I croaked and raised my voice as best I could. "Come on in, Dad." My throat felt like sandpaper.

"How ya doing, son?" he asked.

"Mom phoned you." I seemed to be accusing him of something.

"Sure she did." Dad sounded determined to be cheerful. "She's worried about you. Don't forget, you're my kid, too."

I hadn't forgotten, but I often feel as if he has. I turned my pillow to the cool side and tried to keep tears out of my eyes.

Dad felt my forehead. Then he went into the kitchen, just as if he lived here, and came back with ice cubes which he dropped into my juice. It tasted good. Then he found a washcloth, wrapped more ice in it, and laid it on my forehead. That felt good, too. "Your mother says the doctors tell her there's a lot of this going around," he said as he turned on the TV with the volume low and sat down beside me. The sound and the comfort of Dad being near lulled me to sleep.

When I woke up, Dad was gone, and Mom was smoothing my sheets.

"Was Dad here?" I asked. She assured me he was. For a minute I thought I had dreamed the whole thing. I had never known Dad to act so much like a father before.

January 7

That's enough about my being sick, except to
say that Barry came by with my books, which
he shoved through the window we have to keep
open because of the gas heater. By then I felt
well enough to moan with my eyes rolled back
and my tongue hanging out.

Barry held his nose so he wouldn't breathe
my germs, and Strider poked his snout out the
window. "Hi there, fellow," said Barry, wig-
gling his fingers through the crack. "How's our
dog?" Barry didn't mention reclaiming his custody rights.

I sit here thinking, Please don't, Barry. Let
me keep him. I need him. I don't know why,
but the thought crossed my mind that Barry
was behind in his dog support payments.

January 8

I'm writing all this because I'm bored. As I read what I have written, I see I left out the most important part.

Dad came back another night when I was alone but beginning to feel that I might live after all. He seemed different, not just quiet. Defeated might be the word. I asked, "Something bothering you, Dad?"

He thought awhile before he said, "There's something about a trucker losing his rig that makes him think about a lot of things. Your mother is smarter than me. She's getting her education."

I didn't know what to say to this. Then he asked, "What are your plans for the future?"

That question again, the question without an answer. I said, "Mom thinks I should go to medical school, but I need to earn my own living and not be a burden for years while I go to school."

"Leigh, listen to your mother." Dad ignored my attitude, which wasn't exactly the best. "I'll help you somehow. I'm not lookin' to pump gas all my life. I don't want my kid to make the same mistakes I made."

Dad means well, but I can't count on him. Besides, child support stops when I am eighteen. I just said, "Thanks, Dad."

When Dad left, I felt good because he had come and was concerned about me. I was also a little annoyed because I don't like people telling me what I should do. How do I know I want to go to medical school? I'm pretty sure I don't. Mom is always so sad when a patient dies. On the other hand, she is happy when someone's life is saved. Maybe I just want to bum around the world with my backpack and my bad attitude.

I almost forgot. While I was sick, Barry brought me a box of dinosaur-shaped cookies his biggest little sisters had baked for me. They even frosted them and stuck chocolate chips in the frosting for eyes. Those cookies really pleased me. They also made me wish I had a sister or two of my own.

January 10

Today the weather was good for a change. Although I still feel weak, I have recovered from whatever it was I had. I left Strider at home with Mom, who was studying, and walked, not ran, to school on Jell-O knees and heavy feet. Barry caught up with me. "How come you didn't bring Strider to my house?" he asked.

"The hill was too steep, and I didn't feel that great."

Barry accepted this explanation, which was mostly true. I didn't feel this was the moment to remind Barry he was behind in his dog support payments.

At school, wearing my best attitude, I turned in all my makeup work. My teachers said they were glad to see me back. In English, we worked on an exercise in hyphenated words, which did not take long. Bored, I looked out the window at the pine trees across the playing field, but action on the field caught my attention. A girls' P.E. class was playing volleyball.

One girl, however, was not. Geneva was running hurdles alone. I watched her kneel in an imaginary starting block, take off at the imaginary sound of a starter's gun, and, with an arm and a leg extended, clear the first hurdle, break stride, and knock over the second hurdle. That did not stop her. She ran on, knocking over all but that first hurdle. Then she set them up again and started over. Her hair streamed behind her, and her legs, which I hadn't noticed before, were long and slender. I guess it's sexist to say so, but they are pretty.

I felt old Wounded-hair looking at me, so I pretended to be working. Sometimes I gazed out the window as if I were thinking, when I was really watching Geneva. She knocked down hurdles, set them up, and started over. I had to admire her. She didn't give up.

Watching Geneva, I began to feel better. I longed to be out running with Strider in the cool, washed air that smelled of pine trees, to stretch my legs and extend my stride.

Then old Wounded-hair spoiled my thought by saying, "Perhaps Leigh's next composition should be about the girls' P.E. class, since he finds it so interesting." My attitude toward my

English teacher has gone from bad to worse to worst.

I couldn't help wondering if Geneva had scraped her knees on the hurdles as they fell.

January 12

Barry and I quarreled. I feel terrible.

The quarrel was my fault. When Barry didn't say anything more about Strider, I didn't return him to the Brinkerhoffs' house yesterday on the way to school. I felt so guilty I avoided Barry. I knew it was wrong, but I love Strider so much I made up dumb excuses to myself about how Barry didn't need a dog because he had a full-time father and a bunch of little sisters to keep him company.

Then Barry and I bumped into each other in the breezeway between classes. "How come you don't come by my house on the way to school?" he asked, leaving Strider out of it.

"I guess I'm short of time" was the only excuse I could think of.

Barry scowled. "You almost make me late waiting for you."

"So don't wait." I knew I shouldn't talk that way, but I felt so guilty I couldn't help myself.

Today we met accidentally on the way to school. Barry didn't look exactly friendly. "How come you're keeping Strider?" he asked.

I wished I had a real excuse. "I didn't think you'd care. You didn't pay much attention to him during football season. Besides, he likes it at my house." I hoped this was true.

"Sure," said Barry. "You feed him, but don't forget he's half mine. We agreed."

I said a mean thing. "Then how come you're behind in your dog support payments? We agreed on that, too."

"Why should I pay for a dog you keep all the time?" Barry had me there.

"You pay and I'll bring him back." I didn't know what else to say.

"You sound like you're holding him for ransom," Barry said.

"You know I'm not." I glared at Barry, who glared back.

Knowing I was wrong was making me act so angry. I didn't really want to behave that way, but I didn't know how to turn back. Already I could hear adults saying they knew we couldn't work out joint custody of a dog. They'd have a good laugh, and Strider hadn't done a thing except be a good dog.

Barry started to go on ahead.

"Barry, wait!" I called, feeling terrible.

"Drop dead," he answered.

That made me feel so awful, I was even more angry. "Stinkerhoff!" I yelled and felt like a first-grader.

January 14

Yesterday Barry avoided me.

Last night I felt so heavy inside I had trouble going to sleep and kept one hand on Strider's rough hair as he lay on the floor beside my bed. Once he woke up and licked my hand. I know he likes the taste of salt on my skin, but I pretended he was letting me know he loved me. Maybe he was.

At breakfast this morning, Mom asked, "What's the matter, Leigh? You look down in the dumps."

I told the truth. "I'm just a rotten kid with a bad attitude."

"Oh, Leigh." Mom laughed a sad, amused, worried laugh. "It isn't easy being fourteen."

It sure isn't.

January 16

Barry is avoiding me. He even walked to school a different way, which made me feel so terrible, so tight inside, like the popcorn his sisters shrink back into kernels, that I couldn't concentrate in school and did everything wrong.

After school I walked slowly home, thinking. I had to do something to straighten out this mess. When I opened the door, Strider was so happy to see me he jumped up and licked me. As I hugged him, I noticed he had chewed another corner of the rug.

After I changed my clothes, we went for a run along the edge of the bay. Then we ran around to the butterfly grove, where we walked quietly so we wouldn't disturb the butterflies looking like brown twigs as they clung to the eucalyptus trees. As the sun moved in among the branches to warm the butterflies, they began to unfold and rise in clouds the color of Geneva's hair and to flutter away through the trees.

I always go there when I am sad. Knowing that such fragile creatures can fly as far as Alaska every year somehow cheers me up. By the time we left the grove, I knew what I had to do to make myself feel better.

Back at the cottage, I picked up Strider's correct-posture food stand. "Come on, boy," I said and plodded up the hill to Barry's house, where I set the dish under the overhang of the deck and unsnapped the leash, which I hung on its nail.

When I knelt to scratch Strider's chest, he looked puzzled, as if he knew something was different. I took his head between my hands, looked at his mottled face, his black nose, his alert brown ears, and said, "So long, Strider. See you around." Then I left, fastening the gate behind me. When I looked back, Strider was standing with his front paws on the fence, watching me walk away. "Don't forget me," I called, turned away, and cried.

All this evening I waited for Barry to phone and tell me not to be stupid, to come and get Strider, that we still had joint custody. The telephone just sits there, silent, tan, and ugly. Now I know I didn't really mean it when I gave Strider to Barry. I just wanted Barry to phone and say, "Everything is okay, no sweat, we're still friends."

January 20

Strider's ghost haunts this cottage. The windows are smeared with his nose print. His hair is everywhere. The chewed corners of the rug remind me of the times I left him shut in too long. I seem to hear the click of his toenails on the kitchen floor and the rattle of his license tag, as if he were still scratching. When I go to bed I reach down for the reassuring touch of his rough hair, but Strider is not there.

Today Mom asked, "What's happened to Strider? I miss him."

"He's at Barry's." I tried to act as if this were not unusual.

"Did you boys run into trouble over his custody?" she asked over the rim of her decaf cup.

"Not exactly," I said. "Well, sort of."

Good old Mom. She didn't ask any more questions.

January 25

Funny. Even though I no longer have to exercise Strider, I still have the urge to get up early
and run. Habit, I guess. The first few minutes
I have to push, but as I run, my muscles loosen
up, a good feeling comes over me, and then I
feel as if I am floating.

To avoid Barry, I take a different route to
school. I often meet Kevin, which puts me on
the alert at first, even when I am not wearing
the shirt.

Today, instead of chasing me, Kevin said,
"Hi, Leigh. How's it going?"

"You ask? In the middle of finals?" I laughed
what I intended to be a hollow laugh. At the
last minute I am trying to bring my grades up.

"Make my day. Give me an A." Kevin leaped
up to hit an overhanging branch. "Going out

for track? I've seen you and your dog running around town."

My ex-dog, I thought, and said, "I haven't really thought about it." All I had thought about was Strider, Barry, finals, and sometimes Geneva, the girl with hair the color of monarch butterflies.

We walked in silence until Kevin said, "You know something? Nobody at school ever noticed me until I started chasing you in that shirt. I really liked that shirt, but my mother practically went into coronary arrest when she saw it." He swatted a bush. "I don't mind your wearing it now. At least chasing you in it brought me some attention. People know who I am."

"It's hard being a new kid in school," I said, remembering the sixth grade.

January 26

Today after the math final, I ran into Barry in the breezeway. It had to happen sometime, but he didn't look especially happy to see me, which I thought was unreasonable. He has full custody of Strider. "How come you didn't keep Strider at your place?" he asked.

I wanted to say I was sorry for all the mean things I had said, but harsh, angry words came out: "Because I'm a rotten kid with a bad attitude."

Barry looked as if I had hit him. Maybe if I had done better on my math final, I wouldn't have been in such a bad mood and wouldn't have sounded so mean.

After school Kevin caught up with me. "How about coming over to my place for something to eat?" he asked.

Why not? Without Strider, I didn't have anything better to do.

Kevin lives in one of those big old Victorian houses painted in what they call "decorator colors," which are worth about a million dollars these days. The kitchen was all pink and modern. Kevin opened a door of a huge refrigerator-freezer. "My mother had all our appliances painted this special pink at an auto body shop," he explained, as if he was apologizing. I had never seen so much frozen food outside a supermarket. "Pizza?" he asked. "I'll save the beef stroganoff for dinner. Or maybe the chicken cordon bleu. I'm not into Weight Watchers."

"Pizza's great." I was puzzled. "Doesn't your mother cook?"

Kevin shoved the pizza into the microwave. "She never cooks. We just choose whatever we want and nuke it in the microwave."

While we ate the Pizza, I learned a lot about Kevin, who seemed to need someone to talk to. His father is rich and lives in San Francisco on Nob Hill, or in his condo in Hawaii, and is mad at Kevin because he couldn't get into prep school when practically everyone in the family back to Adam and Eve has gone to prep school. Kevin was mad at his father for divorcing his mother for a younger woman in the midst of the entrance exams he had to take. Kevin ex-

plained that his mother received lots of alimony, and the housekeeper who came in every morning didn't like him to mess up the kitchen. He wished he had gone out for cross-country because it would give him something to do.

I'm ashamed to say Kevin's problems made me feel a little better about mine.

When I told Mom I had a new friend who wasn't very happy, she asked, "What's his problem?"

"He's rich."

Mom laughed and said she wished she had the same problem, but after seeing how Kevin lives, I don't think his being rich is so funny.

Mom said, "Maybe we should ask him over for dinner sometime when I have a day off." Then she added, "Unless you are ashamed of the way we live."

I have never been ashamed, but now I wonder if I'm going to be.

February 13

Today Kevin and I turned out for track. Mr. Kurtz, the coach, gave us a pep talk about the importance of taking part and doing the best we can. He said it's not the winning, it's the competing that's important. He stressed looking for improvement within ourselves. That means I'll have to start chipping away at my bad attitude.

Across the playing field I could see Geneva, arm and leg extended, red hair flying, still working at clearing those hurdles. She is improving, which probably means she has the right attitude.

The varsity team calls Mr. Kurtz "Coach," but most of us younger kids don't feel we know him that well. He watched the freshmen and sophomores work out. Afterward, as we headed for the locker room, Mr. Kurtz put his hand on my shoulder and said, "I have a feeling you're going to make a real contribution to the team. Stick with it." This surprised me. With Barry and Strider so heavy on my mind, my feet felt heavy, too.

To Kevin he said, "With those long legs, you should do well."

February 14

On a scale of one to ten, today was about fifteen. When I came home from school, Strider was sitting by the front door! When he saw me, he came running, jumped up, and licked my face. That long wet tongue felt good.

"Strider!" was all I could say. "Strider!" He wriggled all over, he was so glad to see me.

I looked for his leash, but it was nowhere around. Neither was his posture dish. That meant one thing. Strider had come on his own. The Brinkerhoffs' fence wasn't so high he couldn't get over it if he really wanted to.

I felt great. Strider wanted *me*. I took him inside and fed him in a plain dish. His *slurp-slobber* sounded good, just like old times.

And then the telephone rang. My heart dropped so far it practically bounced on the floor because I had a feeling Barry was calling. He was.

"Is Strider there?" Barry sounded anxious.

"Yes," I said. "Want to speak to him?"

"Wise guy," said Barry. "What's he doing there? Did you come and get him?"

I pointed out to Barry that if I had taken Strider, I would have taken his leash and posture dish, too, and said, "Coming back was Strider's idea. He came on his own." When Strider heard his name, he rested his head on my knee.

"That's what I figured," said Barry, "but I wanted to be sure no one had stolen him."

We were both silent. I could hear the little sisters shrieking in the background, so I knew he had not hung up on me.

Finally Barry said, "You didn't need to give up custody."

"I guess I was upset about a lot of things," I admitted, "so I said things I was sorry for." Maybe it's easier to talk about some things over the telephone, rather than face to face.

"That's what Mom said." Barry was silent a moment while I thought, Thank you, Mrs. Brinkerhoff, for understanding.

Finally Barry said, "You keep him, and I will be his friend. He has shown he likes you best, and I know you exercise him more than I do.

Anyway, I don't like to wash his dish, and he makes my sisters' cats nervous."

"Gee, Barry ..." I was so grateful I could hardly talk.

"That's okay." Barry understood.

When I got hold of myself, I felt I had to mention one worry. "If I keep him, people will laugh and say they knew we couldn't manage joint custody. You know how they talked."

"Yeah," agreed Barry. "They're saying it already. There ought to be some way around all their stupid remarks they think are so funny."

In our silence, I had an idea, a really brilliant idea. "When Mom and Dad got divorced, I heard something about if a kid is old enough and smart enough to form an intelligent preference, he can have something to say about custody. Or something like that. I know I am right about the intelligent preference bit."

"Hey, that sounds great!" Barry was excited. "We can just say Strider is now mature enough to express an intelligent preference, and he decided to live with you." We laughed like old times.

"After all, how many dogs are mature enough to read?" I asked, and we laughed some more. Then I had another thought. "The trouble is, I'm going out for track. I can exercise him in the morning, but if I leave him inside during the day, he eats the rug."

"No problem," said Barry. "Just leave him in our yard like always, and I'll exercise him during track season. I need to stay in shape for football next year."

In a little while, Barry came down the path with Strider's leash and posture dish. We didn't have to say we were glad to be friends again. We both knew it. I also knew, but would never say, that Barry is relieved to be rid of the entire responsibility of Strider. I don't mind washing his dish.

I hugged my dog. Both halves of him are mine!

March 1

The first of the month, I was about to hide Strider in the bathroom before Mrs. Smerling could come demanding rent money. Suddenly I changed my mind. Calling this place a shack gets on Mom's nerves; sneaking around worrying about rent being raised because of my dog gets on my nerves.

Mrs. Smerling's thong sandals came slapping down the path; I opened the door and, with Strider by my side, handed her the rent check Mom had waiting on the chair by the door. "Mrs. Smerling, Strider is my dog now," I informed her. "He has expressed an intelligent preference to live with me instead of living in joint custody."

Mrs. Smerling looked surprised and said, "So?"

"So do you object to my keeping a dog?" I felt a little sick, as if Mom and I were about to become street people.

"You haven't fooled me for one minute," said Mrs. Smerling. "I haven't objected yet."

Whew! I decided to press my luck. "Are you planning to raise our rent because of him?"

"Not unless I have to clean up dog messes."

"You won't," I promised. "I'll get a pooper-scooper or an old license plate or something."

"You're a good kid, Leigh," Mrs. Smerling said. She started to leave, then turned back and asked, "Don't you need a fence for your dog?"

Had she noticed the chewed rug? Probably. "A fence would help," I had to agree.

"So build one," said Mrs. Smerling. "A good fence would add to the value of my property." She went slapping down the path.

Drying her hair with a towel, Mom came into the room. She was laughing. "Leigh, you amaze me. How did you get away with that?"

I shrugged. "By being the man in the family." Now maybe Mom won't miss her little boy so much.

Then Mom frowned. "It seemed to me Mrs. Smerling made a fence sound compulsory."

That was just what I was beginning to think.

March 2

A fence, a fence, my kingdom for a fence, as Shakespeare would say.

The yard already has a fence, overgrown with bushes, along one side and across the back. That leaves the side along the gas station and the space from there to the apartment house in front of our cottage. Barry and Kevin offered to help me build a fence from packing crates from the furniture store down the street, but I have a feeling Mrs. Smerling wouldn't think that kind of fence would increase the value of her property.

Kevin offered to pay for a fence. I couldn't let him do that, and Mom would never allow it. Barry says his father would build me a fence if we asked him. He has all the tools. This was nice of Barry, but I couldn't accept that offer either. I have my pride, even if I don't have enough money for a fence.

Problem solving, and I don't mean algebra, seems to be my life's work. Maybe it's everyone's life's work.

March 12

I got to thinking: if Barry's father would be willing to build Strider a fence, what about my father? Without consulting Mom, I phoned him at his trailer in Salinas. "Dad, would you build me a fence?" No use wasting words.

"Where at?" He sounded surprised. I explained. "Sure, no problem," he agreed and didn't waste time. That same evening he drove over to take measurements by the light from the gas station next door.

A few days later, when I came home from school, I found evenly spaced four-by-fours six feet high set in concrete which had only begun to harden. I pressed Strider's paw into it by the post where the gate will go. Now my dog is immortalized.

Yesterday, when Strider and I returned from

my mopping job, I saw Dad's pickup loaded with lumber, hog wire, a gate already built, and Bandit. Dad was talking to Mom while Mrs. Smerling watched out the window.

"Come on, Leigh. Pitch in," said Dad. Mom said she had a lot of errands to do and wouldn't be home till after work. I think she was just making excuses not to be around Dad.

Dad and I went to work nailing stringers in place. I felt good working with Dad, getting sweaty, while Strider sat watching. Bandit just stayed in the truck.

About the time all the stringers were in place, a lady drove up in a red Toyota, got out, and walked up the path. "Hi, Bill," she said. "How's it going?"

Dad *kissed* her and said, "Great. Alice, this is my son, Leigh."

I remembered to wipe my hand on the seat of my pants, hold it out, and say, "How do you do?" which wasn't easy because I was so surprised. Alice looked a little older than Mom, and plumper, but she was attractive. Nothing flashy.

"Hello, Leigh," she said as if she liked me. She scratched Strider behind his ear when he got up to sniff her over. She said she had errands to do and "just thought I would come by to see how the fence was coming along." Then she drove off.

Suspicious, I asked, "She come to look me over?"

Dad grinned. "Could be."

"You serious?"

"Maybe."

"Any kids?"

"Girl in college."

Old Wounded-hair wouldn't approve of this conversation. Dad and I seemed unable to talk in complete sentences.

By midafternoon, without stopping to eat, we had stapled the hog wire to the fence posts, hung the gate, and screwed the latch in place.

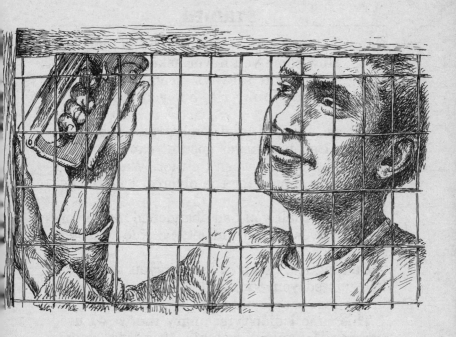

Strider had a neat six-foot fence that should increase the value of Mrs. Smerling's property. I thanked Dad, who said, "That's okay. Let's go get something to eat."

We washed around the edges and, leaving Strider looking surprised behind his fence, went off to a Mexican restaurant where we both ordered the special Mexican platter with enchiladas, chiles rellenos, tacos, refried beans, and rice. Dad had a beer, and I asked for buttermilk, which tasted good with Mexican food.

We ate in silence for a while. Then Dad

rolled a tortilla, looked straight at me, and said, "How come you never asked me for anything before? It always seemed like you wanted a ride in my rig, but you didn't want me."

I was stunned and embarrassed by this speech. Dad was never good at expressing his feelings. Maybe I wasn't either. Wanted him! For a long time after the divorce, I had ached for him.

"I guess I felt you had abandoned me," I confessed, "even if you did let me ride with you sometimes."

Dad sighed. "I know I've let you down, but I've missed you, kid, and I've grown up a lot in the last couple of years."

This time I didn't get angry the way I used to when Dad called me a kid. Now "kid" sounds like an affectionate nickname, not a substitute for my real name, which I used to think he had forgotten.

Dad and I had our first real conversation. I didn't mind so much when he began to talk about my future, although I would just as soon he hadn't brought it up. As he dropped me off at the cottage, he said, "We'll have to build Strider a doghouse."

When Mom came home from work, I woke up and told her about Alice. "Good," she said, and meant it. "I'm really glad he's found someone." Maybe, because he lives so close, she was afraid he would hang around here because he was lonesome. Coming over to build a doghouse is different.

March 13

Now that I have solved a few of my problems, but not my future, my feet feel light. I run faster, as if I had wings on my heels like the Greek god Mercury in florists' ads, except Mercury didn't have to wear track shoes because his feet didn't touch the ground.

Coach wants me to run the eight hundred meters and Kevin to run the fifteen hundred meters. Geneva no longer knocks over so many hurdles.

My days whiz by. Barry runs with Strider after school and brings him to the track for me to take home.

While I mop, I study my Spanish: *Esta mesa es de madera. Está sobre la mesa.*

While I run, I think about the short stories we are studying. This semester's English teacher,

Mr. Drexler, isn't a teacher who pounces on kids trying to look inconspicuous and demands, "What is the theme of this story?" He asks, "Would someone like to volunteer the theme of this story?" because he knows themes are nobody's favorite question. I like to volunteer, even if I am sometimes wrong.

March 14

Today I did a stupid thing. I watched Geneva run the hurdles, and afterward, when she was walking to cool down, I got up my courage to walk beside her. (Not too close.)

"Hi, Leigh," she said.

"Good work," I said, "but did you ever think your hair might offer wind resistance? Maybe if you tied it back, it would help your time." Then I wondered if she would think I had said the wrong thing.

She put her hand to her hair, which curled around her face in damp tendrils. "I never thought of that," she admitted. "Thanks for the tip."

"Your hair is sure pretty," I said to make sure she wouldn't feel I was criticizing. For some reason I thought of Barry's grandmother's beautiful needle-art knitting with soft, colorful yarns. Without thinking, I said, "Your hair would look nice knit into a sweater."

Geneva stopped and faced me with her hands on her hips. "Leigh Botts, you're really weird!" She turned and ran down the track.

I felt like bagging my head.

March 15

Track, track, track.

School is more interesting this semester, especially the study of short stories in English. I study, fall asleep, get up, run with Strider, work out after school. Friday afternoon the team competes against King City in our first meet of the season.

I think of the Olympics on TV: trumpets, sunshine, flags, great-looking athletes from all over the world, the winners struggling to hold back tears when ribbons holding medals are placed over their heads while their national anthems are played and the crowd cheers.

Next to exercising Strider, working out is the best part of the day. I love the grit of my spikes biting into our sandy track, the exhilaration I feel after I run, the satisfaction of cutting down my time. Kidding around in the locker room is fun, even when someone tries to snap a towel at me. I am proud of my gold and red sweats. Geneva smiles and waves at me across the track, so she can't be angry. Barry meets me at the track with my dog.

Sometimes Kevin comes home with me, or we both go to Barry's house. The first time Kevin came here, he blurted, "You mean you live *here*?" Then he apologized for being rude. Kevin has manners.

"Sure," I said. "It keeps the rain off."

Now Kevin likes to come here rather than be alone in a big house while his mother is out playing bridge or, as he says, playing at being an interior decorator. Sometimes we cook. I taught him to make an omelette. If he knows Mom will be home for supper, he wears a necktie! Mom says he's a nice boy with an aura of sadness about him, which must be the sort of boy I was when I was in the sixth grade and my parents were just divorced.

Now I have three friends: Barry, Geneva, and Kevin. I am part of the track crowd. I fit in. I belong.

March 17

My first track meet was about as far from the Olympics as it is possible to get. King City's team is about three times the size of ours. Every kid in King City seemed to have climbed off their buses. Maybe there isn't much to do down there. Wet clouds hung over the field. The two teams piled bottled water, books, jackets, and junk food in separate sections of the cleat-pitted bleachers as if we were staking out territory.

I was surprised at the friendly way members of the rival varsity teams greeted one another. Some mothers and a few fathers, all of them bundled up as if they expected a blizzard and carrying thermos bottles, climbed into the stands.

Runners practiced sprints between the fresh

chalk lanes on the track or twisted and stretched on the playing field. A relay team, all four running so close together their legs looked like pistons, practiced passing the baton.

When the meet started, everyone seemed to cheer for everyone, but I cheered loudest for Geneva, who came in third in the frosh-soph hurdles. I noticed her hair was pulled back and twisted in a knot.

When the loudspeaker blared, "First call, frosh-soph eight hundred," my stomach tightened. I climbed down out of the bleachers to begin my warm-up with the rest of the runners. At the second call, we practiced a few sprints to keep limber, and when the loudspeaker squawked, "Last call," we reported to the starter for our lane assignments.

We peeled off our sweats, took our places. "Runners to your marks. Set." We leaned forward and waited for the starter's gun. A cold wind had come up, making my muscles freeze. I felt a few drops of rain.

Bang! We were off, only to be called back. Someone had made a false start. We were started for the second time. My feet hit the track. The crowd was yelling. Stray words floated into my brain as I stretched my stride: "Hit the road, Jack!" "Put it in high, Felipe!" One lap, and I was still going strong. Coach

was beside me. "Move your arms, Leigh!" he shouted as I passed. I moved my arms and prayed I could breathe to the end of the race. I heard Strider bark. Geneva's voice reached me. "Leigh! Full out, Leigh!" I tried harder as I rounded the curve on the far side of the track, rounded another, and the race was over. A King City guy had won.

I stepped off the track and threw up on the grass.

Coach was right there, his arm around my shoulders. "It's all right, son," he said. "Often happens to beginners. Get your sweats on and keep moving."

After I cooled down, I climbed into the stands to sit beside Strider and Barry. The loud-speaker announced, "Leigh Botts, P.G., third place, 2:27."

"Not bad," said Barry as Strider licked the salty sweat from my hand. "King City is hard to beat."

"Nice try," a varsity runner said. Geneva gave me a thumbs-up. Her hair had begun to fall down around her shoulders.

Two minutes and twenty-seven seconds. When I was running, it seemed forever.

Nobody mentioned my throwing up.

March 31

Run with Strider, school, track, study, sleep, start all over again. That's the way the days go. Cutting my time by two crummy seconds took hours of hard work. I win some, lose some.

Other team members are interesting to watch. There is the good-looking senior pole-vaulter who walks with a swing to his broad shoulders because he knows he will win and all the girls are looking at him, and the varsity eight hundred runner, a real show-off, who is always doing high-stepping sprints in front of the crowd. He has great form; he just doesn't run fast enough.

A girl, a chubby miler on the frosh-soph team, is really fascinating. By the fourth lap, all the other runners have passed her and reached the finish line, but she keeps chugging

along with the whole track to herself. Everyone
watches, nobody makes fun of her, and when
she finishes, a big cheer goes up. I wonder why
she runs a mile when she knows she will never
win. Maybe she wants to lose weight. Whatever her reason, she never gives up. I admire
that.

Bus trips to other schools are fun, with the
team laughing and making jokes on the way
there and sleeping or talking over the meet on
the way back. If the trip is long enough, we
stop at a fast food place on our return. The
varsity team goes in first, with the frosh-soph
team following. Restaurant managers never
look very happy to see us coming.

This morning when Strider and I were running along Ocean View, I saw a sign on Lovers
Point announcing the Annual Lovers Point
Weed Pull, April 1, coffee and doughnuts pro-
vided, and free cypress trees to all participants.
I liked the idea of people volunteering to pull
weeds to keep the cliff along the bay beautiful.
I thought maybe I would pull a few myself. I
owe it to the cliff for being such a great place
to work out.

Today Geneva joined me as I was walking
down the breezeway on my way to our math
class. "You're getting a lot better," she said.
"In track, I mean."

"Thanks," I said. "So are you." When I tried

to think of something else to say, I heard myself blurting, "Would you like to pull weeds
with me tomorrow?"

Geneva stopped so suddenly someone
bumped into her. I stopped, too. She looked at
me as if she didn't believe what she had heard.
"Pull weeds! Did I hear you ask me to pull
weeds?"

I know I was blushing, but I stood my
ground. "That's right." Then I explained about
the Lovers Point Weed Pull and thought, Don't
laugh. Don't tell all the other girls so they can
laugh, too.

Geneva didn't laugh. She answered with a
nice smile, "I think that's a good idea, Leigh.
I'd love to pull weeds with you."

We agreed to meet at nine o'clock Saturday
morning.

This afternoon I sliced three-quarters of a
second off my time in the meet against Gonza-
les and Soquel.

April 1

After breakfast I said to Mom, "Well, I guess I'll pull a few weeds this morning."

Mom sputtered into her decaf. "Leigh Botts! You've never pulled a weed in your life. Whose weeds are you planning to pull?"

"The town's weeds." I spoke with dignity. "On Lovers Point."

"Oh yes, the annual Weed Pull. Good idea. I'm glad you want to help out." She took a bite of nine-grain toast before she said, "Funny, your sudden interest in weeds." I knew she was teasing.

I teased her back. "Yeah, this uncontrollable urge comes over me. Maybe it's seismic vibrations or the position of the moon but I can't help myself. *I gotta pull weeds!*" I tried to look like a werewolf.

Mom laughed. I found an old knife and snapped Strider's leash to his collar.

Mom, who always finds something to worry about, said, "Be careful with that knife." I grabbed a mesh cap Dad once left here, the one that says *A-1 Parts The Truckers' Choice* on it, and ran out the door. "Have fun," she called after me.

I persuaded Strider to walk because I was full of thoughts, such as, Why can't I be handsome like that braggy pole-vaulter? (Actually, I am better-looking than I used to be, but not like that pole-vaulter.) What if Geneva doesn't come, forgets, thinks the whole thing is silly, thinks I'm silly, was just joking? Should I have brought a knife for her, too?

I was relieved to see Geneva coming toward the bench we had agreed on. She's not pretty like some girls, but I thought she looked pretty in a pale green sweat shirt, cutoffs, and a big straw hat. She carried garden gloves and a trowel.

Geneva rubbed Strider's head and said, "Hi, dog." Strider wagged his stubby tail.

The sun was warm, the bay was blue-green, and little waves whispered and swished around the rocks. The air had an iodine smell of kelp. Bees hummed in that plant with giant spikes of tiny blue flowers. All sorts of people of all ages in all sorts of old clothes were digging and pulling weeds. Mr. President's bread truck was parked down the road.

A man from the Lions Club handed each of us a plastic bag and told us he was glad to see young people take an interest in weeds. After fastening Strider's leash to the leg of a bench, Geneva and I went to work digging grass and oxalis out of the ice plant. Oxalis has such pretty yellow flowers, I wonder who decided to call it a weed.

Geneva and I didn't talk much as we dug and pulled, but I did learn that she hurdles because she saw the race on TV during the Olympics, and it seemed like something she would like to do. She lives with her parents (both of them!) in a big old house they have turned into a bed-and-breakfast. Her parents were born in England. Every morning before she goes to school, she puts on a frilly apron and carries breakfast trays to people who order early breakfast. Bursting in on people who are often still in bed embarrasses her. I told her about mopping Katy's floor, something only Barry knows.

A ground squirrel began to flirt its tail just out of Strider's reach. Strider barked and strained at his leash until he coughed, so I pulled out the two cards I carry and held up SIT. Strider looked longingly at the squirrel, but he sat. When I held up STAY, he settled down with his nose on his paws and his eyes on the mean little squirrel who skittered just out of reach.

Geneva sat back on her heels. "Why don't you speak to your dog?"

"What for?" I asked, being funny. "He can read."

Geneva fell over laughing. I took her hand (wow!) and pulled her to her feet. We were both tired and sweaty, so we went over to the truck where the Lions Club was handing out coffee and doughnuts. I had never drunk coffee, but I took the Styrofoam cup the man held out, and so did Geneva. We sat down on Strider's bench to eat our doughnuts and drink our coffee. Strider opened one eye, rested his muzzle on my foot, and closed his eye again. I explained how I happened to own Strider and why he could read a limited vocabulary.

A monarch butterfly wavered along on the breezes and paused on the blue flowers to fuel up for its long flight to Alaska. I looked at Geneva's hair curling around her face and tumbling from under her hat and said, "Did you know your hair is the same color as the wings of a monarch butterfly?"

"Why, Leigh, what a lovely thing to say!" Geneva looked both surprised and genuinely pleased. "All my life people have called me carrot-top. I hate it."

"That's wrong," I said. "You have butterfly hair." Suddenly shy, I looked into my coffee cup, which was still almost full, and said, "I've never drunk coffee, but I guess I was embarrassed to say so. I don't think I like it."

"I don't like it either," said Geneva, "but I didn't want to admit it." We both smiled and emptied our coffee cups in the bushes. An agitated mouse ran out to look and then ran back.

"Thanks, Leigh, for inviting me. I have to go now." Geneva explained that she had to bake cookies because her mother serves tea to guests who are exhausted from all the touristy things people do around here. Her father pours sherry, thickens up his English accent, and acts the part of what is called a "genial host." Geneva says she stays out of the whole scene, partly because people always say they are interested in what young people think, and want to know what she plans to do with her life. She never knows what to say. We agreed that What do you plan to do with your life? is the all-time number-one boring, stupid question adults ask people our age. As Geneva pointed out, we are only fourteen. What do people expect? Our life plans up to the age of eighty?

As we were about to leave, a Lions Clubber insisted we each accept a cypress tree planted in a can, so we could beautify the Peninsula. We thanked him and looked at each other, wondering what to do with our trees.

Mr. President, standing nearby eating a doughnut, was watching us. He understood our feelings because he said, "You're wondering what you're going to do with your graciously received but unwanted burdens." We nodded. "Give them to me," he said, "and in the dead of night by the dark of the moon, I shall plant them in the paths tourists have trampled through native plants on their way to the beach."

"Funny old guy, but nice," remarked Geneva after we handed over the trees.

"A beach guardian," I said. We started to walk, but Strider nipped our heels, so we jogged in silence and reached the bed-and-breakfast much sooner than I wanted. Geneva waved from the porch and said, "See you at the track." Then she went in to bake cookies for tourists.

I have written all this because *this was a great day*.

April 14

Coach says Geneva, Kevin, and I all have times that qualify us to compete in the Rotary Invitational Meet! So long, neglected diary, until the big meet is over.

P.S. Dad phoned to say he has been seeing my times listed in the sports section of the paper. He no longer pumps gas. He drives a forklift for a big produce company and says he will catch up on child support. I've heard forklifters make a lot of money, so we'll see. I would rather have Dad be happy than receive support, but that wouldn't be fair to Mom.

April 29

The invitational meet was held yesterday at our track here in P.G. Today I felt so good I telephoned Geneva and asked her to go running with Strider and me. Kevin was running, too, so the three of us ran together through Pebble Beach and back to Geneva's bed-and-breakfast for something to eat. Mrs. Weston was really nice and made us sandwiches. Geneva's father told us all about how he used to play cricket in England. Geneva winked at us. Kevin and I were polite, even though we really didn't understand what he was talking about.

Tomorrow we have to hand in a composition which I wish I hadn't put off writing until the last minute. Mr. Drexler announced that it must be based on personal experience, which sounded easy until he said, "There is too much fat in the prose written in this class. Too many adjectives and adverbs. Your compositions are to be written using only nouns and verbs."

This brought groans and questions. No, we could not use *the* or *and.* Yes, we could use pronouns because pronouns are substitutes for nouns.

Most of my personal experience lately has been running, so here goes:

"Sun shines, track shimmers, crowd waits. Runners jog, limber, shake arms, test spikes. Timekeeper holds stopwatch. Announcer orders: 'Runners, take marks! Set!' We crouch. I think, Beat two-twenty. Adrenaline rises. Bang! We spring, run. I am front-runner. Feet gaining. Strides match. I sweat. Boy passes me. Crowd yells, 'Go, Leigh, go!' We round turn. Others increase speed. I pass boy. Coach shouts, 'Lift knees, Leigh!'

"I obey, lengthen stride. Boy passes me. Heart pounds, lungs hurt. I pass boy. We round turn. Crowd screams. I strain, strive, turn eyes, see boy. I push, float, see tape. Boy passes me, breaks tape. Crowd cheers. I cross line. I bend, grip knees, pant. Heart thumps. Sweat drips, dots track. I straighten, jog, cool, wait. Announcer gives times. I hear, 'Leigh Botts, P.G., two-nineteen.' I lost race, beat time I set. I rejoice."

There. That finishes my composition, which

does not tell what really happened at the invitational meet, but that is the way I wanted to write it.

I'm pooped. I'm going to bed.

May 2

Yesterday I handed in my composition. This morning Mr. Drexler stopped me in the hall and said, "Leigh, you wrote an A composition, but it puzzles me. I was present at that race. Why didn't you write what really happened?"

I told him I didn't want to brag and have all the kids think I thought I was so great.

Mr. Drexler laughed. "But you have something to brag about. You not only won the race by two seconds, but your time was as good as some of the varsity runners."

"Yeah," I admitted, "but I run to beat my own time, so that is the way I wrote it. Winning is fun, but beating my own time is more important. At least it is to me. You said the composition had to be based on personal experience. You didn't say it had to be true."

Mr. Drexler slapped my shoulder, said, "You're a good kid, Leigh. We're proud of you," and went on into his classroom. I wondered who he meant by *we*.

That invitational meet was so exhilarating it's hard to write the true story without a few fat adjectives.

Geneva was the real shocker. She had cut her hair short.

"Wind resistance," she explained as she handed me a strand of her long hair tied in a bow. "To knit into a sweater," she said with a laugh. I tucked her hair into my gear bag. "Don't look so shocked, Leigh," she said. "My hair grows fast. I've cut it before." She came in first in girls' hurdles, so maybe cutting her hair helped.

Kevin came in third in his mile. He said this would disappoint his father, who had taken an interest in his running. "Since he doesn't have racehorses," was the way Kevin put it. He seemed cheerful about it.

Barry was there to congratulate us. He said he thought he would go out for track in one of the field events next season. The shot put would build up his shoulders for football.

Mom had rearranged her schedule at the hospital so she could come to the meet. She brought Strider with her. Dogs aren't popular at track meets, but she held him on a short leash. Dad was there, too, with Alice. He doesn't look dusty the way he looked a while ago.

I have to admit that feeling the tape on my chest was a real thrill. After my race and all the congratulations, when Mom was talking to Dad and Alice and I was jogging to cool down, Strider jerked his leash out of Mom's hand and came running toward me, dragging the leash along the track. He jumped up and licked my face, not for the salty sweat, I am sure, but because he loves me and knows he is my dog.

Somebody yelled, "Get that dog off the track!"

As I led Strider through the crowd to Mom, I looked down at his rough hair, the way he looked up at me as he pranced along, and I

thought that if someone had not abandoned this great heel-nipping dog who made me get out and run, I might be moping around, feeling sorry for myself.

When I stood beside Mom, pulling on my sweats, I forgot and ordered "Sit!" Strider did not seem to mind the word at all. He sat and looked up at me with a trusting look that told me he knew I would never abandon him.

My dog and I have changed since last summer. After Mr. Drexler's remark about "we" being proud of me, I know that I'll just work to beat my own time until I get wherever it is I decide to go. As in track, I'll probably win some and lose some.

I took Strider's face between my hands, looked him in the eye, and said, "Strider, you truly are a noble beast."

Sorry, Mr. Drexler, sometimes adjectives and adverbs are needed to say what I mean. But in my future, if I become a writer I'll try to keep the fat out of my prose.